DESTINATION UNKNOWN

DESTINATION UNKNOWN

by DALE FIFE

A Unicorn Book
E. P. Dutton • New York

Copyright © 1981 by Dale Fife

Library of Congress Cataloging in Publication Data

Fife, Dale.   Destination unknown.
(A Unicorn book.)
Summary: A twelve-year-old boy stows away on a Norwegian
fishing smack during World War II and shares the harrowing
experiences of its occupants as they cross the Atlantic
to North America.
[1. Sea stories] I. Title
PZ7.F4793De 1981 [Fic] 81-4209
ISBN 0-525-28624-1   AACR2

Published in the United States by Elsevier-Dutton
Publishing Co., Inc., 2 Park Avenue, New York, N.Y. 10016

Published simultaneously in Canada by Clarke,
Irwin & Company Limited, Toronto and Vancouver

Editor: Emilie McLeod   Designer: Claire Counihan

Printed in the U.S.A.
10 9 8 7 6 5 4 3 2

A tribute to my friend

HAAKON SÆTHER
A man of many facets—physician, artist,
writer, botanist—who sailed on the *Bergholm,*
a man who dared to live a life of risk
and high adventure

———————————

for Clare Carey Willard
Mary Theresa Carey
Charles Willard
and the children of Carey School

FOREWORD

Destination Unknown is a fictionalized
account of an historical event. It takes
place in June of 1940 during the Nazi
occupation of Norway. The story is told from
the viewpoint of a fictional character.

CONTENTS

1 Mystery Ship 1

2 Whales in Sight 6

3 Rumors 10

4 Escape 16

5 Galley Slave 20

6 Destination Danger 26

7 Ship at Large 32

8 Overboard 37

9 The Hero 40

10 U-boat 44

11 Moby II 51

12 The Family 57

13 Saint Elmo's Fire 61

14 The Miracle 65

15 The Omen 70

16 Seaman Lunde 73

17 Columbus Again 77

18 In the Jug 82

19 The Modern Leif Ericssons 87

20 From The Battery to Times Square 94

1

MYSTERY SHIP

On the very day the whales were sighted, a strange fishing smack anchored off the Faeroe Islands.

It was June, the time for gathering guillemot eggs. Andy Hansen and I jogged along the quay on our way to watch his older brother, Gunnar, dangle fearlessly over the steep island cliffs.

Suddenly Andy stopped short. "Look, Jon, that smack is not one of ours."

I followed his gaze and saw what looked just like another fishing boat, its crew readying a dinghy to go ashore. It certainly never entered my mind that here at last was my chance to escape to England.

Not many boats put in to the Faeroes these days. "There used to be dozens of them," Andy told me. He knew everything about the islands. I was an outsider.

My home was in Norway. I was stuck here because of the war. I could understand the language since Faeroese is kindred to Norwegian, the Faeroese being descendants of the Norwegian Vikings. But Andy, who was my age, twelve, was my only real friend.

"It's raising a flag," Andy said.

"So what?" I said.

Everything about the islands bored me. I turned away to watch a flock of puffins fly low over the red, blue and green houses. The birds were free. I was caged.

"It's Norwegian, that's what," Andy retorted.

I swung around.

He was right. Whipping in the wind was the familiar red, white and blue flag of Norway.

My throat tightened and I swallowed hard to keep the tears back as I raced to the edge of the wharf.

I knew that Norwegian fishing boats slipped away from Nazi-occupied Norway, sometimes carrying refugees, but they did not come to the out-of-the-way Faeroes.

"She's empty," Andy said, coming to stand beside me.

"How can you tell?"

"She's high in the water. The Nazis probably stopped her and took her catch."

The dinghy was coming in closer. Maybe I'd find out what was happening in Norway. Because of the confusion caused by the war, and the isolation of the Faeroes, it was hard to get news.

I was stranded on Streymoy, in the lonely archipelago which lies between the Shetlands and Iceland, because my father had taken my mother and me with him on a business trip to the Faeroes. My mother, who is American, fell ill and needed medical help not available on the islands. My father was able to get her to London.

"We'll be back in ten days, Jon," my mother said. She hugged me, and the calmness of her green gold eyes made me feel all right about staying alone in this strange place.

My father gripped my shoulders. "You will be safe here. Our friends, the Hansens, will look after you." He showed no fear of the war, of the bombings in England, so I did not fear for them.

That was two months ago. Then Norway was invaded by the Nazis. There was no way my parents could get back to the Faeroes. I had no way of reaching them. I had not heard from them in weeks. I was homesick and scared.

The dinghy was now almost to the wharf. Excitement prickled in me. A husky, red-haired crewman did not wait for the boat to touch the pier. He vaulted easily to the dock and secured the boat.

Two men in the blue uniforms of the Norwegian Navy sprang ashore. One man, a stern-faced officer, wore the gold bars of a commander on his sleeve. The other man, whose quick eyes under thick brows were taking in the whole scene at a glance, had the emblem of a doctor on his sleeve.

The Nazis had ordered all Norwegians to demobilize. Obviously, these officers had refused. Watching them stride briskly up the quay, I felt both pride and fear.

"They're heading for the British headquarters," Andy said.

Five more crewmen began to climb to the pier. Like the one who had secured the boat, they were dressed in the work clothes of fishermen: blue shirts, knit caps, trousers pushed into high boots. Only one was different. He wore plaid knickers and a jacket with a hood, which fell back from neatly combed hair.

A few bystanders had gathered. "How is it in Norway?" someone shouted.

The crew, who had been talking among themselves, fell silent and looked at the man who had been the first on shore. He took his time to answer. "We've come from Scotland," he said, and his face was closed against further questions.

"He's the skipper," Andy said.

"How can you tell?"

"He stands out," Andy said. He pointed to a crewman standing apart from the rest, a gloomy-faced man whose bush of black hair grew low on his forehead. "That's the mate."

"*Kanske*," I mocked. It's the Faeroese word for *maybe*. Andy grinned. "Want to bet?"

I felt let down. I had hoped the men had come from Norway and would have late news. They were now striding toward a shop where they could buy food. The smallest of the crew, a bandy-legged, skinny fellow, whose eyes, behind wire-rimmed glasses, had a startled look, called out to the man Andy said was the mate, "Sven—now maybe you'll get the great cup of coffee you've been grousing about."

Sven scowled. "Anything will be better than the poison you brew."

"Now we know who the cook is," Andy said.

"*Kanske*," I said. "If you know so much about it, tell me why there are naval officers on board a fishing smack."

"Wartime," Andy said. "The navy probably took it over. Come on, let's hurry or we'll miss the egg hunt."

"All right, but let's go by the British office," I said. "Maybe I'll get a chance to see the Norwegian officers again."

We ran the short distance, arriving just as the Norwegians were coming out. I saw right away that something was wrong. The commander's face was beet red. "This is unheard of. An outrage," he exploded.

Still I ran up to him. "Sir, sir," I called. "I'm Norwegian."

He brushed me aside like a mosquito.

The doctor gave me a quick, probing glance and a nod of his head, but that was all.

Disappointed, I kicked at a rock in the road.

"Let's go," Andy yelled. "We'll be late."

I followed, thinking nothing ever went right for me.

2

WHALES IN SIGHT

We climbed up to a windy plateau where a dozen or so of Gunnar's friends, faces toward the sea, toes dug into the turf, pulled on the end of a rope which hung over the edge of the cliff.

Cautiously I moved forward. I got down on my hands and knees and peered below. There Gunnar sat in a flimsy-looking hammock swinging from ropes high above the booming surf. His hands grasped a long rod, at the tip of which was a leather sack. He swung the contraption this way and that, scooping eggs into the sack from rocky ledges. It made me dizzy to watch. I closed my eyes and moved back.

I looked at Andy and said, "I bet they taste terrible."

Andy's blue eyes under his tousled hair were bright as the sea with the sun on it. "You just wait until winter when you get to eat one the way my mother preserves them."

"Not me," I said, pretending to gag.

I have a squeamish stomach, and some of the island's favorites, like raw whale's blubber and air-dried mutton, made me sick. "I won't be here this winter," I said. "I'll be in England."

"*Kanske,*" Andy said.

"What do you mean '*Kanske,*' I yelled, angry at him for hinting that maybe I would not get to England.

Andy stuck his hands in the pockets of his windbreaker and grinned. "How you going to do it?"

"Maybe I'll borrow a rowing boat," I said. "Pack it with all my gear and shove off. I should make Scotland in a few days. From there it'll be easy to get to London."

Andy snorted. "How you going to get through all the mines and subs? You'll get there dead."

"What's the difference? I'm dead here."

I knew it was a mean thing to say. And knew, of course, that the rowing-boat idea was impossible, but I wasn't about to admit it to Andy.

Gunnar's shout to be pulled in jerked me back to the egg hunt. His friends were hauling him, sunburned and grinning, up over the cliff.

Andy and I had the job of packing the big eggs in a basket. They were speckled and ugly. "Why not leave them to the birds?" I asked.

Andy shot me a look which plainly said I was stupid.

I did not fit in to life on the Faeroes. The Faeroese boys were, like Andy, red-cheeked, weather-tough. Even little kids helped with the fishing of cod and herring. I was skinny and my hands were soft.

Andy hung around with me only because I knew things he didn't. He asked questions about everything. He pestered me about America. I had been to the States just once. I was only three, and I didn't remember one thing about it. But that did not stop me from telling Andy tall tales. "Indians with tomahawks hide behind every tree. There are gangsters with guns all over the place."

Andy's eyes opened wide at my stories. Even though his mind was crammed with odd facts, he had never been off the Faeroes.

From the top of the bluff, miles of channel were visible. Gunnar and his friends were just starting down to the village when Andy spied the makeshift flag—a plaid shirt—hoisted on a fishing boat offshore.

"GRINDABOD," he yelled, jumping up and down and waving his arms. "GRINDABOD."

Gunnar and his friends rushed back to the cliff.

"Grindabod," they laughed and shouted to one another.

"What does that mean?" I asked.

"Whales in sight," Andy said gleefully.

"So what?"

"There'll be a whale hunt today. Everything will shut down."

"What's a whale hunt like?" I asked.

"Men in boats chase the whales to the beach," Andy explained. "Others, on shore, are ready with knives and harpoons. It's a bloody sight. Come on, hurry, let's get the eggs home. We don't want to miss any of the fun."

"Ugh," I grunted. "That's fun?"

"It's our food," Andy said, picking up the basket. "Whale blubber is full of vitamins." He smacked his lips. "Wait until you taste a whale steak."

"I can wait—forever," I said.

— 8 —

"Everybody celebrates," Andy said. "We'll get to stay up half the night."

I felt out of it, but I could understand the excitement. Nothing happened on the lonely Faeroes. Even the British being here because of the war made little difference. The islands are scattered. Roads are rough and the sea passages stormy. It takes hours, sometimes days, to get from one island to another.

Suddenly I was overcome by sadness. Were my parents still alive? I thought of our home in Norway—the green valley lined with firs—the splashing stream—the hideaway I had built high in a tree. My aloneness was almost more than I could stand. Whenever it got this bad, I would play my escape game. I began to dream—one day a ship bound for England would come to this very shore. When it left, I would be on it. Even if I had to stow away.

One day it would happen.

How could I know that the day was TODAY?

3

RUMORS

There was a holiday feeling in the air as Andy and I came through the village. Children raced toward the bay where the whales would be herded. Men headed for their boats. Shops closed.

"Too bad this isn't a school day," Andy said. "We wouldn't have to go."

When we came into the Hansen kitchen, it buzzed with activity. Andy's mother stood at the kitchen table frosting a cake. Her blue eyes twinkled. "For the celebration tonight," she said, shoving the bowl over to Andy and me to lick.

Andy's father shrugged into his sweater and pulled his knit cap over his sparse hair. He was heading for the door when Gunnar burst in with news. He had been to the café and met the crew of the Norwegian fishing smack. "They're not talking much, but the town is filled with rumors."

"What about?" Mr. Hansen asked.

"They say the boat is on a dangerous mission. It's so secret that not even the crew knows where the smack is going. The two naval officers are supposed to have volunteered in England, and were sent to Scotland to board the fishing boat."

Mrs. Hansen looked up from the bowl of meat she was chopping. "Where could they be going?"

"Nowhere," Gunnar said.

"What does that mean?" Mr. Hansen asked.

Gunnar snitched a piece of the meat. He talked around it. "The skipper told us they stopped here for oil, but even as he was telling us this, the two naval officers came into the café. The captain—the crew call him 'Stoneface' behind his back—was boiling mad. The British had refused the oil."

"REFUSED!" Mr. Hansen exploded. "They can't do that to an ally."

"Well, they did. I heard the captain say so."

"It makes no sense," Mr. Hansen said.

Andy was licking the frosting spoon. "Why do you call him 'captain'? He has a commander's stripes."

"He's in charge of the boat, that's why," Gunnar said.

"I thought the skipper has charge of a boat," insisted Andy.

"Not when the navy commandeers it," Gunnar explained. "Then the navy officer plots the course, but the skipper remains in charge of the crew."

Mrs. Hansen shook her head. "They are so far from Norway—from home. Sad."

Gunnar looked pleased with himself. "I invited them to the celebration tonight. They're mostly young fellows. The skipper agreed that they could use a good time, and the captain accepted for all of them. They'll be sailing sometime after midnight, he said.''

"Where to?" Mr. Hansen asked.

"Without more oil, they have no choice," Gunnar said. "They have enough to get back to Buckie in Scotland, where they started from. The captain said he and the other officer would go back to England and report the failure of their mission. He looked very angry.''

ENGLAND!

I gasped.

Here was the chance I had been waiting for.

My legs felt wobbly.

Mrs. Hansen stared at me. "What's wrong, Jon? Don't you feel well?''

"Not very," I said.

She went to the sink, washed her hands, then set the tea-kettle on the stove. "Go upstairs and rest," she said. "So you can enjoy the fun tonight.''

Mrs. Hansen was good to me, although I suspected she felt I was a spoiled weakling compared to her boys.

I went up to the room I shared with Andy. Mrs. Hansen followed with a pot of tea. She fussed around the room while I drank it.

"Will you be all right alone?" she asked.

I thought she must be anxious to be off. Andy had told me that the women would not take part in the hunt, but with the children they would stand on the shore and watch, or they would gather in the meadow where the celebration would be held.

"I'll be all right," I said.

After she left, I sprang to the window which framed the

harbor. A telescope on a tripod stood in front of it. I focused it on the fishing smack.

She was maybe sixty feet. There was a sleek look about her. The steering house, aft, had four windows across the front, with none of the usual bulky look of most steering houses. I picked out the letters that spelled her name— *B E R G H O L M*. And underneath it— *N O R W A Y*.

Schemes flicked about in my head.

How could I manage to be on her when she sailed? Captain Stoneface or the tight-faced skipper would never tolerate me on the boat. I would have to stow away. But how would I even reach the boat? There was no one to row me.

I could swim.

Could I make it?

Kanske!

How would I carry dry clothing?

I had a waterproof bag.

Food?

Plenty in the Hansens' larder. I'd need only enough for two or three days. It would not be stealing, because my board was paid.

With two navy officers and six fishermen on the smack, where would I hide? Could I keep from being seen? My stomach churned at the thought of being discovered by Stoneface.

The crew looked to me to be a tough, hard-muscled bunch. Most of them were two or three years older than Gunnar. Sven was probably older. He made me shiver. As for the red-haired skipper of the *Bergholm,* he looked as if he'd throw me overboard if he found me.

Was my scheme possible?

Kanske!

Did I have the nerve?

I wasn't sure.

The house had now settled itself to a creaking quiet. Everyone was gone. I padded downstairs and rummaged for the things I needed.

I found cheese and flatbread. There was wind-dried mutton, but one whiff of the dark, hard meat and I knew I'd rather starve. I did like Mrs. Hansen's rhubarb jam. Rhubarb was one of the few things besides potatoes that grew on the island. I took a jar of it, even though it was heavy. I'd always wanted to have a whole jar to myself.

Back in my room, I kept uneasy watch on the *Bergholm* while I rolled up a blanket, clothes, and food, and what money I had. Then I packed the lot of it in my waterproof bag. I could see the men at work.

Getting ready to sail?

Plans changed about going to the celebration? One moment I wished they would leave. The next I prayed they would stay.

It was late afternoon when I saw the dinghy pulled up close to the fishing smack.

My mouth felt dry as a blotter as I waited.

Then the men climbed into the little boat.

They were coming ashore.

My insides fluttered as I watched the dinghy draw alongside the quay. The men jumped ashore and started toward the meadow. Even at this distance I sensed they were ready for a good time.

This was my chance.

My fingers shook as I wrote a note to leave on Andy's pillow:

When you read this, I'll be on my way to
England to find my parents—if I can get
on the *Bergholm*. I'll write as soon as I
can. Tell your folks not to worry.

                                        JON

P.S. About the Indians and gangsters—
I never saw one.

Picking up my gear, I went outside and started along the
back road. I could hear music from the meadow and laughter
in the distance, but I didn't see a soul.

When I reached the wharf, it was deserted.

Out there was the *Bergholm*.

Now all I had to do was swim to it.

I thought of all the things that could go wrong.

I was only a fair swimmer.

Even if I made it, how could I hide from so many men?

"GO BACK!" something told me. If I don't make it, if I
have to call for help, I will lose face with the island boys.

If I go back now, no one will ever know.

Go back?

4

ESCAPE

I took one last look at the *Bergholm*.

She rode proudly, bow to the sea, scorning the land, as if daring me to take the chance. In less than a week I could be in England.

The windows of the steering house flickered flame in the late evening sun. They blinded me. Ripping off my shirt and pants and stuffing them into the waterproof bag, I tied it securely to my swim trunks and plunged into the sea.

The shock of the icy water numbed me. Madly I thrashed to get some feeling in my legs and arms.

The boat, which had seemed so close, now looked beyond reach.

I had been a fool. Not only did I have to reach the boat, I must try to hold up my bag in case it was not truly waterproof. It held all my survival supplies.

I swam on, pushing with legs like lead. The boat seemed to get no closer.

My whole body felt numb, when my foot cramped. I cried out in pain.

Give up?

Yell for help?

I panicked.

In that terrifying moment I caught a glimpse of the blazing windows of the *Bergholm*.

They were a beacon.

Floating, I pushed my good foot against the cramped one and treaded water.

I went on.

Each stroke brought me closer to escape.

At last it was an arm's length away.

Breathless, I reached out, grabbed the anchor chain and hung there exhausted.

When my heart stopped pounding and I could breathe, I grasped the anchor chain with both hands to pull myself up. It was slippery with slime and seaweed, sharp with tiny shells that cut into my hands.

I slid back.

I tried again. My hands were raw but I was getting closer to the rail.

One more inch.

Hold on.

Pull! One more time.

At last one hand on the rail—then both hands.

I hauled myself up over the rail and tumbled onto the deck and into darkness.

After a while I opened my eyes. I looked up at a blue sky. I heard the slosh of water. I felt the sun.

Where was I?

I was on the *Bergholm*! I had made it!

What was that sound? Hammering!

There was someone on the boat besides me.

I grabbed my gear and stumbled aft, frantically searching for a place to hide among coiled ropes, canvas, boxes.

In my rush I knocked over a can. It rolled along the deck and came to rest by an empty oil drum lying on its side, held by blocks of wood.

I crawled into the drum. Something soft moved beside my face.

I held my breath.

A CAT.

I'm allergic to cats. I sneezed.

Heavy footsteps.

Coming closer.

Black boots right outside the drum.

STOPPED.

Another sneeze was about to burst.

I pressed a finger under my nose, and gave the cat a shove out of the drum.

A growling voice: "Oh, it was you, Trouble."

I recognized the growl. It belonged to the man called Sven.

"You're bad luck, Trouble," he grumbled. "All cats are bad luck."

The footsteps went on, but I was still afraid to move. I shivered.

It was cold. I opened my bag and felt like shouting. Water hadn't touched anything. I changed into dry pants and shirt. Then I spread my blanket along the side of the drum.

After a while, Trouble came back.

I didn't care for cats, but she had saved me from being caught. She settled onto a burlap sack.

"You can share my blanket," I told her. "After all, it is your house." She ignored me, and with her claws began to knead the old sack.

I opened my packet of food and offered her some flatbread. She sniffed at it and turned her head away.

"Good," I said. "Now I can have it all to myself. I hadn't expected company."

She yawned. Her eyes were a gleaming green, and her coat was tiger. She was fat. "Do you eat too much, or are you expecting kittens?" I asked.

She ignored me, settled down with her paws under her chin, closed her eyes, and purred.

I heard the sound of waves against the hull, the creaking of the ship. My eyes got heavier and heavier.

I did not know how long I had slept when I was awakened by the grating of the anchor chain, the sputtering of the engine, the sound of voices.

The boat shuddered and jolted forward.

We were under way.

I snuggled into the blanket. I told myself, "All is well!"

But was it?

In two or three days we'd dock in Scotland. Another day and I'd be in England.

Kanske flashed through my mind.

I shook my head to deny it and dropped off to sleep.

5

GALLEY SLAVE

A strange rumbling-rolling awakened me. I felt cramped. I stretched my arms and legs as well as I could in the drum.

Something was missing. The noise of the engine.

We were stopped. I heard water slosh against the hull. Voices. The screeching of gulls.

Scotland?

Impossible. I could not have slept that long.

Cautiously I stuck my head out. I saw a metal drum, much like the one I was in, being rolled across the deck toward me.

I pulled back.

Now there were more voices. More rumbling. My hiding place was being surrounded by so many drums that it was completely dark inside. Safe!

I edged out. Over the tops of the drums I glimpsed the heads of some of the crew.

The captain took off his cap. "All right now," he said. "We'll pool our money to pay for this oil."

I watched as the men reached into their pockets and tossed money into the cap.

Someone snorted. "So the British were going to keep us from getting oil. Lucky this side of the island doesn't know what's happening on the other."

"Silence!" the captain said. "Quislings are everywhere."

Quislings? Those traitors!

WE ARE STILL RIGHT ON THE FAEROES!

If they found me now, they would put me ashore. I crouched as far back in the drum as possible. The cat came in and snuggled up to me. Her smooth, warm fur under my fingers comforted me, but I was afraid I'd sneeze any second.

It seemed forever before I heard the putter of the engine, the bump of the boat against the wharf. Voices. Orders. We were on our way.

There was nothing to do but hide and sleep. I had slept so much I didn't see how I could sleep anymore.

I squirmed and wriggled, trying to get into a comfortable position without my legs sticking out of the drum. At last I fell asleep.

The cramping of my muscles awakened me and I became aware of a ghastly feeling in my stomach. I pushed hard against it with my arms. It made the awful feeling worse.

The boat pitched forward.

Trembled.

It rolled from side to side.

Whatever it did, my insides did the same.

The odor of Diesel oil floated around me.

The cat sat at the opening to the drum just by my feet. She had a dead fish in her mouth. I was going to be sick. I had to get out. In a hurry. Dragging myself out of the drum, I staggered to the rail and clung to it, heaving.

My head spun dizzily.

Which way was back to the drum?

An iron hand landed hard on my shoulder and held me fast.

I looked up into the face of the mate—Sven.

"What's this?" he shouted. "Hey, Ruud. Come here."

A giant of a man with a tough, weathered face vaulted over an oil drum and took a good, hard look at me. "OHO! So you caught a fish. Hey, Thompsen!" he shouted to a man in the rigging, "look what the sea coughed up."

Thompsen scrambled to the deck. He was a short man with a mashed-in nose. He grasped my arm with steel-like fingers. "Is it real?" he asked.

"Let go of me," I yelled.

"It speaks Norwegian," Thompsen said. "It is a Norwegian fish. What will we do with it?" He bared pointed teeth. "Let's cook it and eat it."

"Too puny," Ruud said. "All bones. I say we should throw it back into the sea."

Sven glowered at me. "Stowaways are bad luck. Take him to the skipper. He's at breakfast."

Ruud grabbed me, lifted me over his head like a stick of wood.

I yelled. I thought he might throw me overboard.

He carried me into the cabin and slammed me down on my feet. The man with the reddish hair, whom Andy had said was the skipper, sat at the table between two lower bunks.

His jaw dropped open and he half rose in his chair at the sight of me.

"A stowaway," Sven said.

I was going to be sick again. I gagged.

Ruud let go of me. I ran up and leaned over the rail.

I was sick until I thought there could be nothing left inside of me.

The iron hand was on my shoulder. Sven dragged me back to the cabin and stood me before the skipper again. The doctor was seated beside him now, and the skinny one called Olaf was pouring coffee into mugs.

"What shall we do with him?" Sven asked.

Olaf squinted at me through his thick glasses. "He could be a dangerous spy," he said.

"The captain will question him," the skipper said. He turned to the doctor. "What's your recommendation for seasickness?"

The doctor's face twitched. "The seaman's treatment."

"Olaf," the skipper said. "Pea soup for our sick passenger. Keep giving it to him until he stops puking."

At the thought of it, my stomach churned. And when the awful greenish liquid was set in front of me, I shook my head. "No," I yelled.

"Yes," the skipper said.

I swallowed a spoonful and ran out to the rail.

All day I drank pea soup.

All day I ran to the rail.

I was sorry I had been born.

I hated these men. Most of all I hated Sven and Ruud and

the doctor. I despised the miserable *Bergholm* with its perpetual motion.

That evening, even though the sea and my stomach had calmed down, I felt as if I had been drowned and wrung out to dry. How could I live until England?

I sat beside the empty cat drum. Even Trouble had deserted me. It was time for the evening meal. No one called me. I didn't care. The smell of fish cooking was horrible.

Sometime later, Olaf came with stale bread. "Doctor's orders," he said.

I turned up my nose at it.

"Dry bread is good for a sick stomach," Olaf said, pressing it on me.

I threw it to the sea gulls trailing the smack. They caught it in midair.

"Shows who's hungry around here," Olaf said. "You don't have to eat, but you do have to go before the captain. He said I was to bring you to the wheelhouse."

That scared me, but I wasn't about to admit it. "Old Stoneface?" I said.

The cook rolled his eyes. Behind his glasses they looked enormous. "Ever been flogged?" he asked.

I thought he was making fun of me, but wasn't sure. I got up and followed him.

The captain was very busy over charts. The doctor was standing by one of the windows. They both ignored me for some time. Finally the captain turned to me. His face did indeed look as if it were carved of stone. Nothing moved in it except his eyes, which were like chunks of blue ice. "What are you doing on the *Bergholm*?" he demanded.

I want to reach my parents. I was stranded on the Faeroes."

"Your name?"

"Jon Lunde."

"Age? Nationality?"

"Twelve. My father is Norwegian. My mother is American."

"American, so you're spoiled."

I bristled. "I was in America once. I was only three."

"Whatever you are, you are spoiled. You have stolen onto a working boat, so now you will work." He turned to the cook. "Olaf, this boy will help you in the galley."

He must be joking. "I have money to pay my way to England," I said.

"ENGLAND!" he exploded, and turned to the doctor. "He thinks we're headed . . . This is going to make it worse, taking a boy along. . . ."

The doctor nodded. "We can't go back. Nothing can be done about it now."

Olaf nudged me down to the galley. Sven was in the small room pouring himself coffee.

"Where are we headed?" I asked Olaf.

He shrugged.

"I'll tell you where," Sven said glumly. "Davy Jones's locker."

"There's no such place," I said.

Sven's eyes narrowed. "So you know it all! Well, let me tell you, you'll be with Davy Jones if we meet up with a mine or sub."

6

DESTINATION DANGER

The *Bergholm* bucked and plunged and leaped through the sea. I slaved in the galley.

The galley was not much more than a cubbyhole. Olaf could stand at the cookstove and, with his long, skinny arms, reach the cupboards on three sides. When he peered through his glasses and groped for salt or flour, or whatever, he looked like a nearsighted octopus.

One of my first jobs was to take a huge pot of coffee to the table at breakfast. From the galley at the bow to the cabin aft it was a slippery walk along the pitching deck. My arms strained under the weight of the pot but I somehow made it through the door.

Since there were eight men and only four bunks, the crew "hot-bedded." Those on dogwatch slept days. The men on daytime duty crawled into the bunks at night. Only at mealtimes were most of them gathered together.

By now I had sorted out the crew. This particular morning, besides Sven, there were Thompsen, the machinist, Ruud, the motorman, and Kristiansen, who always looked neat and clean even when doing hard, dirty work.

He was no fisherman. Olaf had told me that Kristiansen was a patriot and worked in the resistance.

Just as I hoisted the pot to the table, the boat heeled. The heavy pot slipped from my hands, hitting the table, and the lid popped off.

In horror, I watched a stream of coffee spread along the table. The men had put their caps under their plates to keep them from sliding when the boat lurched. Before they could snatch them away, the coffee flooded them. Sven, who was sitting at the far end, got coffee over his trousers. He jumped up so suddenly his head hit the upper bunk. His face was distorted with rage. "Are you a boy or a goat that you can't carry coffee?" he shouted.

"He's a galley goat," Rudd said, grinning. "A-a-a! A-a-a! A-a-a!"

The nickname stuck.

After that, everything that went wrong was blamed on me.

"The Galley Goat must have cooked the oatmeal today. The lumps are as big as goose eggs," Thompsen complained.

"Galley Goat, do you think you can bring more bread without spilling it?" Ruud shouted.

This caused such loud laughter that the skipper stuck his head out of his bunk to see what was going on.

I soon learned that it was up to me to do all the mean jobs on the boat. I had to see that the fishing tackle was coiled up neatly and that the long lines of fishing hooks and the bait were in order, even though we did not stop to fish. Sven was a Simon Legree about it.

The worst job was emptying the garbage pail. Each time I lugged it to the deck, I gagged. After the evening meal on the third day, I held my breath to keep from smelling it as I stumbled out to the rail and swung. I forgot about emptying it with the wind, I was so anxious to get rid of it. The boat, which had been leaning to starboard, shifted to port, and I shifted along with it. Garbage flew through the air. Sven, who was on his knees tightening a rope, was showered with potato peelings and fish heads.

He raised a fist. "Clean it up, Galley Goat," he shouted.

Instead, I ran to the cat's nest, humiliated that I could do nothing right and enraged at the way I was treated.

Trouble crept into the drum, arched her back and snuggled down beside me. The cat was the only living thing that liked me.

I was still feeling sorry for myself when the doctor poked his head inside. "Only the sick can stay in bed on a fishing boat," he said.

"I'm sick of the boat," I snapped. "I hate it. And everyone on it. You all make fun of me."

"The men have to have something to joke about," the doctor said. "Forget it, and so will they."

I didn't answer, but after he left I crawled out of the drum. It was still light as day for this was the land of the midnight sun. Kristiansen was standing close by looking up at the wheelhouse, where the crew were gathering.

Olaf ran by. "The captain's going to break the seal on the radio," he said.

"Let's see what's happening," Kristiansen said.

In the wheelhouse, the men crowded around the radio. The captain explained: "The British sealed the radio so subs could not trace our beam. We haven't seen any subs. It's time we learned how the war is going."

The skipper interrupted. "It's unlawful to remove the seal."

"The *Bergholm* is my responsibility," the captain retorted. His cool gaze went from face to face. "It's time you know what our mission is."

He paused. The only sound was the *slap-slap* of the waves against the hull. "As you know, our king and his cabinet fled to northern Norway. We are going to try to reach them."

The room erupted.

Norway! HOME. My home was in a small place called Støren, midway between the north and south.

I shivered with excitement and fear.

The skipper held up his hand for silence. "That's laying ourselves wide open to the Nazis. They're patrolling the Norwegian coast. They've laid mines."

The captain's face was stonier than ever. "True. But not only have we the Nazis to contend with, we are an unidentified boat. If the British should spot us east of the Greenwich meridian, they'll probably take us for Nazis and blow us right out of the sea. The doctor and I have important papers. We must cross the Greenwich meridian. Is any man afraid to try to reach the coast of Norway?"

"*NEI! NEI!*" the men shouted.

A satisfied look passed over the captain's face. "I thought the truth would make you stubborn men more determined than ever."

At first, after the seal was removed from the radio, we heard only static—weird noises—until finally a far-off thread of words pierced the wails and howls:

BBC—BBC—LONDON—

As the men huddled closer, tense, the words faded and were lost.

Suddenly a voice, strong, clear:

BBC—LONDON—ADAMS SPEAKING —CRITICAL ANNOUNCEMENT—ALL OF NORWAY HAS NOW FALLEN TO THE NAZIS. KING HAAKON AND HIS CABINET HAVE BEEN SUCCESSFULLY EVACUATED FROM NORTHERN NORWAY. THEY ARE HERE IN ENGLAND WITH US.

The news and the stunned faces of the crew paralyzed me. I had been hoping the war was over. Now all of Norway was gone. We could not go there.

The captain was the first to speak. His face was as unreadable as ever. "This explains why the British were so uncooperative on the Faeroes," he said.

The doctor nodded. "Too bad they couldn't tell us."

"Probably didn't know themselves," the captain said. "Wartime orders. Secrecy."

Sven groaned. "We'll all be buried at sea."

The captain and the doctor exchanged glances. The captain went to a cabinet and took from it a heavy envelope. It was about twelve inches square. "There is burying to be done," he said. "These are the papers we were to take to Norway. Our orders were to sink them if we could not deliver."

He said it matter-of-factly. Then, with his usual vigorous haste, he went below to the main deck.

We all followed.

I was the last. I thought the captain was rightly named Stoneface, for even now he showed nothing in his face.

But at the rail he shook his head. He could not seem to let go of the envelope.

The doctor, standing beside him, took it and, reaching low over the rail, let it slip from his hands.

To me, the envelope was Norway itself. I pushed in between the captain and the doctor. "It's gone. I can't even see it now," I cried.

"It was weighted with lead," the doctor said.

I felt as if Norway now lay dead, buried in the sea. I wiped my eyes with the sleeve of my jacket.

Behind me I heard Sven: "That's where we'll all end."

"Enough," the captain said. "The bad news we have heard changes everything. Every man not on duty inside for a meeting."

Silently we filed into the cabin, seven of us waiting for the captain's words.

Surely this means the *Bergholm* goes back to Scotland.

Now I will get to England!

7

SHIP AT LARGE

Sunlight shone through a porthole and flickered across the captain's hard-jawed face as he stood before the men. His first words were cold as doom. "We are now a ship at large. We have no place to go. In such a situation the rule is: Every man shall have his say as to what we shall do."

The skipper jumped to his feet. In the shaft of sunlight, his red hair blazed like fire. "We were told by the British in the Faeroes to go back to Scotland, where the smack and my crew came from."

"Foolhardy," the captain said stoutly. "With the Nazis now holding Norway, our way back would be through a sea of mines, with subs lurking everywhere."

Kristiansen, usually the quietest of the men, spoke up. "I say act boldly. Sneak back into Norway. It is my hope to again work for the resistance."

"Suicide," the captain spat out. "If we wish to be of further help to Norway, we must not act rashly. We must think of how to save the *Bergholm,* as well as our lives."

The doctor calmly raised a question. "In what port would we be welcome?"

"Tahiti?" Olaf shouted, swiveling his hips.

This brought chuckles.

It broke the tension, but only for a moment. Sven's voice growled through the room. "A boat without a country! We'll flounder until we sink."

The doctor repeated his question. "In what port would we be welcome?"

The captain's gaze moved slowly from man to man. "I say we have only one choice left. West!"

"West!" the skipper gasped. "How far?"

"Until we hit North America," the captain shot back.

The men smiled. It was a joke, of course. Only the skipper took the remark seriously. "Impossible," he said. "Our charts do not extend that far. How can we find North America?"

The captain spread his arms wide. "It's a big continent. How could we miss it? Canada is part of England, and I hope we can land on British soil."

"CANADA!" Sven said, choking on the words.

The skipper looked at the captain as if he thought he had lost his mind. "How can we go to the other side of the world in a fishing smack?"

"A very strong smack," the captain said, admiration in his voice.

"True," the skipper said, "but do we have adequate instruments? We have a sextant, but no charts for the other side of the world."

Thompsen shook his head. "We are fishermen. What do we know of the seas beyond here?"

The doctor went to his books and brought one to the table. "I carried my old school atlas with me when I joined my unit. I thought to mark the map to show our forward progress. Instead, as you well know, we progressed backwards at such a pace there was no time for marking." He opened the atlas to a folded map of the world, which he spread out on the table. We crowded around.

The captain put his finger at a point on the coast of Norway. "We are here, opposite Tromsö," he said. Then with his thumbnail he made a crease on the map to show the route to North America.

I followed the route—well below Greenland—across the North Atlantic—past Newfoundland. "Here is Nova Scotia," the captain said. "I would hope we would hit somewhere along this coast."

Sven's voice rose above those of the other men. "How about Nazi subs?"

The captain shrugged. "Yes, there is that danger, but the Nazis are not going to bother with a fishing smack unless they suspect it is carrying wanted refugees or men from the Norwegian underground. But if we should be boarded, all of you realize that the doctor and I must not be found. As Norwegian officers who refused to demobilize, you know what the Nazis would do to us. And now we will vote."

He turned first to the doctor.

The doctor ran his fingers through his thick black hair. When he raised his head, he spoke without hesitation: "As a doctor, I am needed in England. I so vote."

The captain nodded. He did not comment. He turned to the skipper.

The skipper's face was bright with excitement. "America. I never expected to get there. I'm not sure we'll make it, but I so vote. Let's go west."

To a man, the crew held with their skipper.

"Six ayes and one nay," the captain said. "Even if the crewman on duty votes nay, the ayes have it."

The doctor pointed a finger at me. "The boy's life is also at stake. He should have a vote."

With a wave of his hand, the captain dismissed the idea. "He is not a member of the crew."

I felt myself flush with anger. But I said nothing. There was planning to do. Sven was glum about the oil and food supplies. His somberness began to infect the crew.

It was now that I saw another face of the doctor. His craggy features softened. I could guess he had voted for England out of a sense of duty. But now that we were heading west, he plunged into the adventure with a reckless disdain of fear which caught on with the crew, despite the gloomy Sven.

I felt out of it, so helpless and useless, so apart from these seamen, that I hurried out on deck and to the cat's drum. Trouble was sitting on top of it, sunning herself. I thought of what lay ahead for me—thousands of miles of seasickness perhaps. I looked out at the lonely sea. Empty. No ships. Nothing. I was faced with living for weeks with eight men who despised me. One of them—it was Ruud—was deftly climbing high on the rigging, scanning the sea with binoculars. I thought he was probably trying to spot mines or U-boats. The mast swayed gently, but he moved as one with it. It was Ruud who had slung me over his shoulder like a matchstick and carried me before the skipper. It was Ruud who had given me my nickname of Galley Goat.

— 35 —

I thought of my home in Norway and my tree house. The climb to my shelter had been easy for me. Reaching the tip of the mast would be just as easy. Suddenly I felt challenged. I must prove to myself that I could do something as well as Ruud.

The big man climbed down. He stood on the deck, hands on hips, looking up at the mast, as if pleased with himself. I thought I'd like to have the feeling of being pleased with myself, to feel pride.

Until I had climbed that mast I would not rest.

Now was the time.

I ran toward the mast and was on my way.

8

OVERBOARD

I got halfway up when, from below, they started yelling at me.

"Jon, come down," Ruud shouted.

"The boy's crazy," Sven's voice carried up to me.

The more they shouted, the more determined I was to climb high enough to grab hold of the topmast.

I made it.

I looked down.

I was lord of the ship.

Looking up at me were Ruud and Sven and Thompsen.

Now the skipper was below, shouting up at me, "JON, I ORDER YOU DOWN."

Instead, I began to climb even higher on the thinner spar.

I was excited. Exhilarated by my success.

Suddenly, the wind seemed to come at me from all sides.

This mast was different from my tree at home. That had rough bark to dig into. The mast was smooth. Slick. It began to sway back and forth in a larger arc—larger—LARGER. Each time the boat heeled over, the mast dipped and the sea rose in sickening swells.

I knew I must go down.

But now the deck seemed far away.

There was a sudden violent lurch of the boat.

"HANG ON," the men shouted from below. "HANG ON."

I tried but I couldn't.

I lost my grip.

I was flung far from the mast, headed for the waves below, and I struck the water with such force it knocked the breath out of me.

DOWN I went.

UP I came.

DOWN.

UP!

KICK. TREAD WATER. FLOAT!

WHERE is the boat?

Far away . . . LEAVING ME!

Can't they see me?

YELL!

Salt water in my throat.

Choking.

Something grabbing hold of me! SHARK? Fight!

A voice: "Easy now—easy." RUUD! Close beside me.

I could hear the boat's *chug-chug*. I saw now that it was coming closer, heeled toward us.

Hands reached out.

It heeled the other way and I sank in the trough of a wave.

Hands disappeared.

Water in my eyes, my ears, my throat.

The boat heeled toward us again—a life preserver splashed—hands—voices—

Shaking, freezing, I was hauled to the deck.

The doctor half carried me to the cabin. He gave me a going-over. "Get on dry clothes," he ordered.

Olaf burst in. "Ruud. We've got Ruud. He looks bad."

As I went groggily out of the cabin, I saw Ruud. He was gray-faced, bent over in a convulsion of coughing.

"Get him into bed," the doctor ordered. "We don't need pneumonia."

The hostility of the crew was apparent.

Away I slunk to the cat's drum.

But no cat.

Never had I felt so alone. So despised.

9

THE HERO

Ruud did not get up the next day. At supper the hoarse breathing coming from his bunk seemed to fill the cabin.

No one, not even Olaf, spoke to me.

After the meal, as I cleared the table, the doctor sat studying the map in his atlas.

Ruud broke into a spasm of coughing. It hurt me to hear him.

"Is it because of me?" I asked.

The doctor's eyes were probing. "Why did you do it?"

I swiped the dirty dishrag across the table. "To show that I can do something besides empty the garbage, scrub the decks, peel potatoes—all the jobs no one else wants."

"Ah, I see. You want to be a hero."

"Not exactly, but I don't like being a slave."

The doctor took a toothpick from its container. He broke off one small tip and tossed it onto the blue of the ocean on his map. "If that were the *Bergholm,* what odds would you give that it would make it across to America?"

"Sven says we're going to sink," I said.

"It's possible," the doctor said. "But Sven is working his shirt off while he says it. Jon, there are no heroes on this boat. It is the *Bergholm* herself that will see us through. She's in a contest with the sea—a sort of tug of war, you might say. She will win if the crew is good enough. We're a team—the *Bergholm,* the officers and the crew, doing anything to make her win. Any job, well done, counts."

I knew he had signed to take Ruud's watch. As he stood up to go, his gaze went to the greasy streaks I had made on the table with the dirty dishrag.

My face burned. I escaped to the galley, where a mound of dishes awaited me, and heated a dishpan of water. For the first time, I really washed the dishes so they did not feel greasy. Then I scrubbed the boards of the table. My hands were raw, but somehow I felt better after that.

I went up to the wheelhouse. The doctor was at the helm. "Is it hard to steer a boat?" I asked.

The doctor gave me a quick, appraising glance. "You can learn the mechanics quickly enough," he said. "The most difficult time is when you think you see something unusual in the usual. Then you must make a decision. Is it real, or just a mirage?"

I saw nothing but water. All that was between us and Canada was water—water—water.

Although it was almost midnight, the sun was a great brass coin in the wide sky. The sea was quiet. I had an eerie feeling that there was nothing in the entire world but the *Bergholm,* and the only people alive were the eight strangers with whom I had thrown my lot. I had a queer sensation that I was standing outside my skin, looking at a ninth stranger—myself, a gawky, useless kid.

Sea gulls suddenly swooped low over the boat, and the strange feeling passed. I began to think and wonder about the long journey ahead. "I'm puzzled," I said to the doctor. "How can we find our way without charts or instruments?"

Thompsen came just then to take the watch. The doctor slipped from the seat and motioned me along with him to the cabin.

He poured two mugs of coffee. No one had poured coffee for me before.

"Jon," he said, sitting up to the table and motioning me opposite him, "now about your question regarding instruments. You might say we are making the second discovery of America."

"Columbus had some instruments," I said.

"But what do you think Leif Ericsson had a thousand years ago?"

"If he didn't have instruments, how did he know where to go? How does the captain know how to steer?"

"The captain is an experienced navigator. He has been in many waters. He knows direction. He has a watch, a compass. He looks at the sun. He knows without charts where he is—not exactly, of course."

"We could get lost then."

The doctor nodded. "True. Still, by dead reckoning he knows how far he has come. He knows what his longitude is. He measures the speed of the boat at least once each day and computes the distance."

"It's a long way for a little fishing smack to go," I said.

"Yes, but the *Bergholm* has already proved herself. She's had some tough missions in this war. She's what the sporting people call 'yare.' "

"What does that mean?"

"She responds quickly and truly to the helm."

I went out on deck. I felt the *Bergholm* plow the waves—steadily—endlessly. To me, she had been a way to get to my family in England. I had not thought of her as anything special.

Yare. A new word to think about. *Yare*. The sound of it gave me a good feeling. The *Bergholm* was not just an ordinary fishing boat. *Yare* was like having heart, I thought. She would get us to America. We would not end up in Davy Jones's locker.

America.

A faraway, strange, unknown place.

What would I do there?

What would happen to me?

How would I get back home?

Would I ever find my family again?

Slowly, but surely, the *Bergholm* was taking me farther and farther from everyone and everything I knew. That thought was even more frightening than the sea.

10

U-BOAT

"PERISCOPE TO STARBOARD."

The warning came at dawn.

Quick steps.

Orders.

I rolled out of the cat drum, still groggy with sleep, and I sat there, paralyzed.

I tried to remember the skipper's instructions. What were they?

"Should we be boarded," he had told us, "the captain and the doctor must disappear. As officers who escaped rather than obey the Nazi order to demobilize, they would be put in prison or shot if discovered."

After the explanation, he had told each of us what to do.

He had looked straight at me. "Don't open your mouth.

They'll know immediately that you don't belong on a fishing boat.''

Just as I got to my feet, Sven came, shouting, ''Run! Into the cabin.''

Then I remembered. My job was to stuff the captain's and the doctor's uniforms into waterproof bags.

Glancing to starboard as I ran along the deck, I could see nothing.

When I burst into the cabin, the captain and the doctor had already stripped off their uniforms. I snatched them up.

Where were the waterproof bags?

Under one of the bunks.

With shaking hands I hauled them out and shoved the uniforms into them.

The engine stopped.

Ruud crawled out of his bunk to help tie the bags around the waists of the officers, who then scrambled out of the cabin and to the rope tied to the port side rail.

I stumbled out, just in time to see the doctor and then the captain climb over the rail, slide to the water and grab hold of the rope loops fastened at the waterline.

I hung over the rail but I could not see the men because of the bulge and the inward curve of the boat's side.

''Away from the rail,'' Ruud yelled hoarsely.

As I wheeled around, I saw the periscope. It was coming at us, slitting the water like the fin of a killer shark.

I felt as if an icicle had been shoved down my throat as I watched the U-boat, some fifty feet away, thrust its bow up from the depths—a giant monster with dripping jaws. The *Bergholm* rocked back and forth violently.

A hatch cover opened atop the submarine. An officer and

three able-bodied seamen climbed out of the hatch. The seamen pointed rifles at us.

A rope ladder dropped down the side of the sub.

An officer—he had the stripes of a lieutenant—shouted an order in German through a megaphone.

Our skipper, hands on hips, shook his head.

The lieutenant repeated the order in Norwegian: "Lower the dinghy and approach the U-boat. We will use it to board you."

The skipper's face, when he turned to us, was expressionless. He gave the order: "Sven! Thompsen!"

Petrified with fear, I watched the lowering and the rowing of our dinghy to the sub. The German lieutenant and a seaman climbed down into it and were rowed back to the *Bergholm*. I watched the boarding—first the seaman with the rifle; then the lieutenant, who did not move from the gunwale, although his sharp gaze missed nothing.

Our skipper stood forward of the crew, who lined up behind him, silent, hands at their sides.

The Nazi beckoned to the skipper, who moved toward him reluctantly, slowly.

"Where do you come from?" the lieutenant demanded in perfect English.

I knew that the skipper understood some English. I also knew it could be a trap by the lieutenant, suspecting British on board.

The skipper shook his head.

"Woher kommen sie?" the lieutenant repeated in German.

Again the skipper shook his head.

Now the lieutenant spoke in Norwegian, poor Norwegian. *"Hvor kommer de fra?"*

"We are fishermen from Måløy," the skipper said.

I held my breath. We had not been near the Norwegian fishing village.

"Your papers," the lieutenant ordered.

"You are far from Måløy," he said when he had read them. "Why are you in these waters?"

"We fished off Iceland," the skipper said.

The lieutenant's eyes narrowed. "The fishing, was it good?"

"Fair," the skipper said.

The lieutenant's eyes were challenging. "Show me your catch."

We had no fish. What would the skipper do now?

He shrugged. "A German cargo ship ordered us ashore. They took our fish."

"They did not leave you even one fish?" the lieutenant snapped.

"That's right," the skipper said.

I clenched my teeth to keep from chattering. Would the lieutenant believe the story?

The seaman with the rifle had been prodding at everything on the deck—the nets—the stores—lockers. Finally, he gave the signal that he had found nothing suspicious.

The Nazi officer then left the rail and strode to where the crew was standing. I stood at one end, next to Ruud. Trying to look like a real crewman, I pulled my stocking cap low over my face.

"Any refugees on board?" the Nazi asked.

"No," the skipper said.

The Nazi stood for a moment before each man, scrutinizing him. When he came to me, his eyes seemed to bore right through me. He yanked off my cap. I knew I looked like what I was—a scared twelve-year-old boy.

"What's a young boy doing on this fishing smack?" the lieutenant yelled.

I ground my teeth together to keep my chin from trembling.

"SPEAK!" he ordered.

I didn't dare.

Ruud put a hand on my shoulder. "He is my son. He is frightened and seasick."

The German turned away from me to watch the man with the rifle, who was now walking along the port rail, looking over the side. He was getting close to where our captain and the doctor had slid to the tow loops.

There was a sudden swell.

The ship heeled hard to starboard.

Were the captain and the doctor visible with the ship heeled over? Were they still holding on to the tows, or had they had time to submerge? How long could they stay under?

The seaman started to bend over the rail to look down.

I ran toward him, gagging, pretending to be sick, bumping into him.

He turned toward me.

And then I was really sick—all over the Nazi seaman's shoes—over the deck.

The seaman screamed something at me.

"GENUG!" —*enough*—the German lieutenant ordered.

He gave a small salute to the skipper, handed him back his papers, and then swung over the gunwale to the dinghy. He was followed by the seaman, who gave me one last sour look where I had collapsed on a heap of canvas.

"We were lucky," I heard the skipper say. "The officer

was not one of the Hitler gang. He was correct, polite enough.''

By the time I got back on my feet, the skipper and the crew had brought Sven and Thompsen back on board and hoisted the dinghy to the deck.

They were jubilant that everything had gone so well.

"Now it is safe to bring the captain and the doctor up," the skipper said.

Olaf hurried to the galley. "We will have a celebration. I'll cook the last of our bacon."

I felt miserable. The only thing I had thought to do was play sick, and then I really had been sick. What a mess.

I slunk to my refuge—the cat's drum—and almost crawled over a small creature.

Two small creatures.

Sitting back on my heels, I saw that Trouble had had her kittens.

"Couldn't you pick a better time?" I groused as I backed out.

Now there was no place for me to sleep.

The engine began to stutter. It took hold. We were on our way again.

When I next stuck my head into the drum and sorted out the occupants, I counted four kittens.

"Meow," Trouble complained, as if I made one too many in the drum.

I picked up the biggest of the litter—a gray and white striped ball of fur. Its eyes were closed, but its claws were sharp. "You'll need those claws," I said, "to get along on the *Bergholm.*"

I sneezed: "KACHOO!"

"That's a good name for the kitten."

I looked up.

The skipper.

I scrambled to my feet.

"Congratulations," he said. "You did some fast thinking with your seasickness."

The unexpected praise made me self-conscious. The only thing I could blurt was, "Trouble's got a drumful of kittens. Where will I sleep?"

The skipper grinned. "I don't allow my crew to sleep in drums. We'll find a nest for you."

I felt like swinging from the halyard and shouting to the skies. At last, did I really belong?

Was I really a member of the crew of the *Bergholm*?

11

MOBY II

Sea gulls trailed us constantly.

"They think the *Bergholm* is a smorgasbord," Olaf complained to Kristiansen and me one evening as he threw leftovers to them. Potato peelings were about all they got.

We watched the constant wheeling of the birds and listened to the *swish* of the water slipping past. "The gulls glide in concert to a silent rhythm," Kristiansen said.

He was always saying things like that. "He is a poet at heart," the doctor had told me. "One day he will be heard from."

Olaf looked up to the mast and the gull that had taken possession of it days ago. "He thinks he owns the mast," he said.

"Maybe he wants to be the first to see America," Kristiansen said. "I say we should christen him 'Columbus.' "

So Columbus he was.

The farther we ranged from the land, the fewer the gulls. "The gulls tell us about the weather," Sven said one day as I helped him stow gear. "I don't like to see them leave."

"How can a gull tell you anything?" I asked.

"He is the fisherman's barometer," Sven said. "See how low he flies. He can soar only when the pressure is low. When it changes, he knows instinctively. If there is a gale, up he rises to glide on the wind."

I was never quite sure whether the men were joking when they talked to me about the sea. But now I hoped the gulls would stay.

But day after day, the gulls dropped back, until one morning there was only Columbus left, standing, as usual, on the top of the mast.

I threw one of my breakfast pancakes into the sea. He flew down and gobbled it gratefully. I was glad to be rid of it. Olaf's pancakes were like stove lids.

Sven caught me at it. He came at me, scowling. "The day will come when we starve on this boat and you will wish for that pancake."

I laughed. "How can we starve?" I asked. "There are fish all around us."

"So you will have us stop in the middle of the Atlantic to fish," he shouted at me. "We should go this way and that, hunting fish while we use up our fresh water and our oil. There are nine of us on this smack, and whatever provisions we have must last until we reach land. Otherwise there will be nine dead ones." He turned his angry face toward Columbus. "If you are a smart gull, you will follow the others."

The next morning, Columbus was gone.

I felt uneasy. Did gulls know when to desert a boat?

I began to feel guilty about being on the boat. I was eating, and sometimes wasting, the crew's supplies. I'd have to learn to eat fish cakes and "stove lids."

Although the gulls had deserted us, comical little birds by the hundreds surfed along the ocean swells. In their black and white feathers, they slid and tumbled down the waves like circus clowns. Sven and the skipper had a running argument about them. "They're puffins," Sven said.

"Murres," the skipper said.

I asked the doctor about them. "They're a kind of auk." The doctor always knew the scientific names of things. "*Uria* genus," he added.

Some days wild geese flew over us in military formation, reminding me of Messerschmidts I had seen over Norway.

Porpoises came in great numbers to romp around the bow of the *Bergholm*. They leaped high into the air, then arched gracefully back into the sea, playing tag. When I mentioned this to the doctor, he grinned. "They're not always playing. They're mammals. Sometimes they have to come up to breathe." Maybe so, I thought, but it still looked like fun.

One morning, as I scrubbed down the deck, Kristiansen called me from the rail. He handed me binoculars. "Look over to starboard. There's a sight you won't often see."

At first I saw only spouting geysers.

"WHALES," I yelled when I made out a huge shape leaping high into the air.

Some of the crew gathered and took turns looking through the glasses.

"I'd say there are fifty," Thompsen said.

"More like a hundred," Sven argued.

"They're smart," I said, "not to hang around the Faeroes and end up as whale steak."

Whale talk continued through breakfast.

"Those whales are probably finbacks," Thompsen said.

"Or sperms," the doctor said. "They travel in large family groups."

"A whale is a whale," Sven said. "They're just too big to come close to a smack."

I set more bread on the table. "Are they dangerous?" I asked.

"When they get in the way," Sven said. "Once a whale rolled right under a boat I was on. We almost capsized. I was knocked off my feet."

The doctor raised an eyebrow. "I'll bet that scared the whale as much as it did you."

"You should have seen that whale," Sven went on. "It jumped high out of the water. I swear its dorsal fin was as tall as our mast. Only thing worse to meet up with is a sea serpent."

Now I knew he was telling a big one. "There's no such thing," I said.

Sven glared at me. "What does a boy know?"

"Tell me," I mocked. "What does a sea serpent look like?"

"You'll know one if you ever are unlucky enough to meet up with a sea serpent," Sven shouted at me, then clamped his mouth shut and turned away.

Afterwards I asked the doctor. "Have you ever seen a sea serpent?"

"No, but I am not a true sailor. I'm just a war sailor."

"Do you believe Sven saw one?" I asked.

The doctor's eyes twinkled. "I believe he thinks he saw one."

I thought of stories I had heard about sea serpents—how they wrapped their tentacles around fishing smacks and crushed them to pulp. I was a war sailor too. I would not believe.

Yet Sven did. And his life was the sea. But Sven was always looking on the gloomy side of things. I wouldn't believe the whale story either.

But I wasn't so sure the next morning. When I came into the wheelhouse with coffee for the skipper, a whale was rolling ahead of us. It looked as long as the *Bergholm,* and as scary as the U-boat that had stopped us.

"Can't you get out of its way?" I asked.

"The whale knows we're here," the skipper said. "We'll confuse it if we suddenly change course. It'll leave when it gets ready."

To Sven's alarm, the whale stayed with us—now trailing—now alongside—now diving. Sven's worries communicated to me. Maybe the whale was under our boat and would turn us over. When it broke water, it looked as big as a railroad boxcar.

The doctor said the whale was a sperm.

"How can you tell?" I asked.

"By its boxy head. No other whale has a head shaped like that."

"Why is it staying with us?"

"Probably it's as curious about us as we are about it."

"Maybe it's hungry," I said.

"It's got plenty of squid and fish. The sperm is a roamer."

Kristiansen came alongside as we talked. "Moby Dick was a sperm," he said.

"Hi, Moby II," I called down to the whale.

I thought the whale understood, for it rolled over, flipped its tail and showed off a bit.

"Sven is afraid it will capsize us," I said.

The doctor nodded. "It could, with one swish of that tail. It's an especially big sperm. It probably weighs sixty tons, but it has very good hearing and knows exactly where we are."

"I hope it stays with us all the way," I said.

Kristiansen shook his head. "Don't get too attached to things, especially whales."

The same day, after supper, I heard a strange sound, like that of a giant stringed instrument sounding one long, drawn-out note. I ran out to the rail just in time to see Moby II shoot a plume of spray skyward. Then the whale rolled away from the boat, leaped high out of the water and dived. It flipped its giant flukes and was gone. It was like a good-bye.

The doctor had told me that sperms could stay underwater for an hour.

I watched until the stars came out.

Moby II never came back.

12

THE FAMILY

I no longer slept in the cat drum. My quarters had been upgraded to a nest of blankets in a corner of the cabin.

But every morning, first thing, I would go to see Trouble and her family.

The kittens had names now. Kachoo was the biggest. Olaf had called the feisty one U-boat, after the German sub; and we named the reddish one Skipper, because his fur was red, like our skipper's hair.

My favorite was Bright Eyes. She was the runt of the litter, with a face so tiny that her eyes loomed huge and bright. It was Bright Eyes who was always getting into mischief. She hated the oil drum, and either Trouble or I was always chasing after her and rescuing her from one hazard or another.

This particular morning was sunny with a warm wind astern. As I reached the drum, Trouble came around one of the other drums carrying Bright Eyes in her mouth. She walked over to me and dropped the kitten at my feet and left her.

"Hey," I called. "She's yours. Not mine. Maybe I have spoiled her a little, but she's too young to leave her mother."

She was a tiny ball of tiger fur, warm and soft against my cheek. She settled on my shoulder and purred.

Just then the skipper came out on deck, yawning and stretching. "Hey, Jon, how about breakfast?"

I had forgotten that Olaf had the night watch. Breakfast was up to me alone.

I put Bright Eyes into the drum and headed for the galley.

Stoking the fire took time. A little wood, some coal, then a spray of petrol. But after several tries, I had the tiny stove roaring and coffee bubbling in the big pot.

Olaf had taught me to brace myself against the bulkhead while I sliced hunks of bread, and I knew how to hold down the clattering lid of the oatmeal pot with an iron weight to keep it from flying off when we wallowed and rolled.

We no longer had eggs, but there were sausages and flatbread.

The captain and the doctor often came to table together. I had made friends with the doctor, but not with the captain. I was always afraid I would do something wrong when Stoneface was around, yet he made no more demands on me than on the crew. His speech was spare. Even when he was not in the wheelhouse, I had the feeling that his thoughts were there, figuring how to outmaneuver the sea.

Thompsen came bursting in. "It's a fine day," he shouted, as if we were all hard of hearing. "A good day to wash. My socks are standing up by themselves. Jon, how about heating up a bucket of water? Shave in some yellow soap."

"Be sure you're using salt water," the captain said. "The skipper tells me we're low on fresh."

"Salty socks," Thompsen exclaimed. "Well, salt never hurt a sock."

I didn't tell him we'd been boiling the potatoes in sea water for some days.

After breakfast, I hauled up a bucket of sea water, heated it and dragged it out on deck, along with a washboard I'd found.

When Kristiansen saw what was happening, he brought more sea water to be heated. While Thompsen washed only his socks, Kristiansen scrubbed all the clothes he owned. He was the "dandy" of the crew. The captain and the doctor shaved every day, but Kristiansen was the only crew member who did. The rest sprouted beards like pirates and only occasionally clipped off the bristles.

Washday was catching.

Soon the rest of the crew brought out their laundry. Plaids and stripes, clothes of every color, hung from the ship's rigging and stretched on lines from the steering house to the cabin door and between the masts.

I added my two shirts and two pairs of socks to the collection. The sun was warm on my bare back. It didn't take long for the clothes to dry.

The skipper said it was a good day to put up sail. "A fair wind. We'll save a little oil."

Olaf brought out goat's cheese and apples.

We sat on the deck to eat.

The *slap-slap* of the sail in the breeze, the talk and joking of the crew, all made for a feeling of well-being.

It's like a picnic, I thought.

The last picnic I had been on was with my parents in Norway. Had they heard from the Hansens about my stowing away on board the *Bergholm*?

I began to think about how they would worry about me if they knew I was on a fishing smack in the middle of the Atlantic. I had acted thoughtlessly, and I was sorry.

And yet, strangely, my parents now seemed unreal. The Hansens, even Andy, were like phantoms. Only the *Bergholm* seemed real. It was as if nothing existed besides the fishing smack, the nine of us, and the cats.

I decided the cats should be at the picnic. I went to the cat drum and fetched them.

I put Bright Eyes on my shoulder. She snuggled up to my ear. I could hear her tiny heartbeat.

We were a family. A world to ourselves.

13

SAINT ELMO'S FIRE

Now I felt like a real seaman, taking my turn with the rest of the crew doing any job necessary. Hands calloused, and my face windburned, I had my sea legs. Feeling as vigorous as the sharp, salty air I breathed, I could devour with gusto whatever Olaf dished up.

I hung out in the wheelhouse as much as possible. I never tired of watching the helmsman steer through, around, and sometimes under the waves that raced toward the *Bergholm*.

The perpetual motion was lazy at times, boisterous more often, and sometimes so violent it raised the hull to shivering heights, then threw it down hard on its bottom. A bump on my head big as a gull's egg proved I had hit the top of the pilothouse.

But I wasn't scared anymore.

One morning, when the doctor was at the helm, and I was

polishing brass in the wheelhouse, Kristiansen came in with a gash on one hand. The doctor beckoned to me. "How about taking over?"

I looked around, thinking another crewman had come in. It was clear he meant me.

I scrambled onto the helmsman's seat and grasped the wheel.

The doctor pointed to a number on the scale of the compass. "Keep her there all the time."

I grappled with the wheel.

"Not so anxious, Jon. If it sways a little, put it back gently."

Slowly, I began to feel the wonder of this new sensation. Through my fingers, I began to sense the inner workings of the *Bergholm*. I felt the strain on her ribs, the beat of her heart. What excited me most was her spirit. She did not plow. She rode the sea. I began to relax my hold, to give the *Bergholm* her head. She responded to each touch. I felt a part of her.

Long after that short stint at the wheel, the thrill stayed with me. I asked questions of the crew and lost myself in the stories they told about the *Bergholm*.

She was only nineteen tons, but she had fired the first shot against the Nazi invasion of Norway. Like many fishing smacks, she had been pressed into patrol duty. I listened excitedly as one evening after supper the captain told the story.

"It was three in the morning when we met three big cruisers, five destroyers, and an auxiliary fleet. I ran the *Bergholm* close enough to the leading cruiser and hailed her. Answering in perfect English, they said the ships were British, 'sent by request of your government.' However, since they showed no flags, I ordered her to heave to, so that I might board her. She ignored the order. I fired a shot across her bow.''

The captain paused for a moment. I couldn't wait to hear the rest. ''What happened then?'' I asked.

''She replied with a broadside but not at us. They were Nazis sent to shell the Norwegian shore. We escaped by a miracle.''

There were other exciting stories. After the invasion by the Nazis, the *Bergholm* made many dangerous trips spiriting Nazi-marked resistance men and women out of Norway. I was thrilled to be on the *Bergholm*. She would get us to where we were going.

I had forgotten one thing—the power of the sea.

One evening as I took food to Trouble and the kittens, I saw a bluish ball of fire atop the mast. I dropped the food and raced back to the cabin, where some of the men were playing a game of cards. ''The mast is on fire,'' I yelled.

My news was greeted with grins all around.

Feeling foolish, I backed out of the cabin and ran smack into Sven, staring up at the flame. His face was even more solemn than usual.

''What is it?'' I asked.

''Saint Elmo's fire,'' Sven said.

''I never heard of Saint Elmo,'' I said.

''Well, you'd better make his acquaintance. He's the guardian of the sailor. That fire up there is a warning that we're in for bad weather.''

As usual, when I was puzzled, I sought out the doctor. He raised an eyebrow at my question: ''What causes the fire on the mast?''

''Easily explained,'' he said. ''Electricity discharges from the high points on ships—often when bad weather is ahead.''

"But Sven said it's a warning from Saint Elmo that there's a storm coming."

The doctor thought awhile. "As far back as the Romans and Greeks, sailors believed that twin balls of fire foretold fair weather, and that one ball foreboded danger."

"There's only one," I said. "Do you believe that Saint Elmo is warning us?"

The doctor's lips twitched. "Sven does. He's the seaman."

14

THE MIRACLE

I went back to Trouble and the kittens. As usual, Bright Eyes was wandering. I went looking for her. As I scooped her up from behind one of the oil drums, I heard a ghostly hissing sound. It came from the blue flame. Something about it made me shiver.

Bright Eyes squirmed in my hands. I scolded her for not staying with her mother, even while I petted her and felt her warm fur against my face.

The weather was changing. Fast.

The wind roared through the rigging.

I carried Bright Eyes to the drum. Trouble and the other kittens were already inside. "You stay there," I told Bright Eyes as I shoved her in with the others.

As I started forward, the *Bergholm* rolled like a rocking horse.

"Squall," Ruud yelled.

Already in his yellow slicker, head bent into the wind, he shouted at me: "LIFE JACKET!"

I stumbled into the cabin. By the time I got into the bulky jacket and came back on deck, everything loose was rolling. It was as if a hurricane were whirling right under our hull, dragging us into a roaring hole one moment, then tossing us high on the edge of a foaming cliff the next.

Sven was trying to secure a boom. He was only a foot away, but when he cupped his hands and shouted something at me, I could not hear for the shriek of the wind and the wild sea roar. He thrust a lifeline into my hands and pointed to the cabin. I understood I was to lash myself onto something there.

I shoved the lifeline into a pocket and started to obey the order when I remembered the cats.

Hanging onto anything I could grab, I made my way aft. I had to stop every few steps to catch my breath through sheets of spray. My eyes smarted, my chest hurt and my fingers ached with wet and cold. The slippery deck climbed and fell away under me.

Something hit me. It was the cat drum, broken loose from its blocks of wood, rolling back and forth crazily across the deck.

In horror I saw that Bright Eyes was half in, half out of the drum.

I crawled toward her on my hands and knees, and was within an arm's length when we slid into a trough and the sea crashed down over us. It washed my kitten to the edge of the gunwale, just below the rail.

Her forelegs were spread wide—her little claws extended.

I reached up to grab her.

Another wave smashed over the boat.

The kitten's eyes were black with fear—then she was gone.

I lay without moving.

The drum rolled toward me. I grasped its edge and held on. I managed to pull out the burlap sack. Somehow I got Trouble and the three remaining kittens into it. Dragging it, I crawled and staggered back to the cabin.

Water splashed from one side to the other. Books, papers and clothing sloshed about.

I dumped the sack into a locker, hoping the cats wouldn't smother. They could not survive on deck.

Suddenly I realized that in all the wild sounds of wind and water, a sound was missing.

The engine's throb.

I clung to a bunk frame, listening, waiting.

Was the engine room flooded?

Ruud and Thompsen were the engine experts. Could they get it started?

I had never felt such fear as I did now.

I could not stay lashed in the cabin, alone.

A wall of water washed over me as soon as I groped my way back on deck.

Clawing, crawling, I made my way across the deck and into the wheelhouse. Reeling and choking, I fell against the skipper. He grabbed me and put me between him and the wheel just as the whole foredeck went down into the sea.

When we came up again, I got out of his way. He was as if welded to the *Bergholm,* the two of them fighting the sea.

I heard the captain: "Port side's against the weather."

Even I knew that without the engine, the skipper could not turn the *Bergholm.*

I would never see my parents again. They would not know what had become of me.

I felt terror at the thought of dying.

A shudder went through the *Bergholm*.

Was she splitting apart? She was shaking violently.

THE ENGINE! It was the engine!

The *Bergholm* regained its balance.

The skipper was in control.

We lay right, aft to the weather.

A silent cheer rose in me.

What could I do? Bail?

Making my way from the wheelhouse to the deck, I heard a shout: "ON GUARD!"

Squinting through the spray, I could not believe what I saw.

Ahead of us, directly in our path, a mountain, floating in ghostly foam, was moving toward us.

"ICEBERG!" shouted Sven.

A current dragged us closer. And closer.

I heard a grinding crunch. The *Bergholm*'s bow rose up out of the sea onto the berg, throwing me to the deck.

A monstrous wave engulfed the boat and wrenched us off the iceberg. Our boom was torn from its moorings.

The boom slammed into one of the crew. Visibility was almost nil and I could not tell who the man was. He rolled helplessly down the sloping deck and was lodged close to where I clung to the rail. He did not move.

I crawled toward him.

Sven! Unconscious.

It was not possible to drag him. Another deluge would wash him overboard as easily as it had my kitten.

I groped for the lifeline Sven had given to me. Somehow

I managed to tie it around his legs and to the rail. Then I clung to him.

Was this the end?

Would the *Bergholm* sink?

Through the shrieking storm I heard the beat of her engine. How long could she go on?

In all the violence, that beat now became a part of me. I heard nothing else.

Slowly, it became louder and began to rise above the storm.

Sven stirred.

Gradually, the storm eased up.

The *Bergholm* had won the battle.

Our hull was not crushed. The iceberg had just brushed us.

Sven, who had had the wind knocked out of him, came to quickly enough. We were both exhausted.

I glanced up.

Twin balls of fire flamed from the mast.

Sven grunted. "Fair weather ahead."

"Thanks, Saint Elmo," I said.

Now I believed. As strongly as Sven.

15

THE OMEN

The next morning everything was gray—the sky—the sea
—the men.

The *Bergholm,* coated with ice and salt spray, looked like
a ghost ship. Her deck was a shambles.

The men were cold, wet, hungry and suffering from
bruises and sore muscles.

The galley stove stood deep in water.

Our world was grim.

And then the bird came. Not an ordinary bird. A red and
gold, beautifully striped bird, perched on top of the cabin
entrance.

Kristiansen spotted it first. He motioned to Olaf and to me.

"What kind is it?" I asked.

"A sparrow," Olaf said.

"Sparrows are brown and gray," I said.

Olaf squinted up. "I call all birds that size sparrows."

Everyone came to look at it.

How did the bird get here?

How had it lived through the storm?

Even the doctor could not identify it. "I've never seen a bird like it."

Sven, who was usually worrying about something, smiled. "Any bird who could live through that storm must be a good omen."

"Maybe it's hurt," I said. "Maybe it's hungry."

"It's resting," the doctor said. "When it feels strong again, it will be on its way."

Even as he spoke, the bird spread its wings in a rainbow of color and flew away.

We all felt better because of that bird.

"I wish it had stayed," I said.

"No," the skipper said. "The cat might have caught it."

Sven turned a sad face to me. "Trouble is gone. The kittens, too. They must have been washed out to sea. The drum is empty."

"They're in a locker," I shouted and raced to the cabin.

I was almost afraid to open the locker. Maybe the cats had died.

But as soon as I grabbed the sack, I heard angry meowing and felt sharp claws through the burlap.

I hurried back on deck and let the cats loose.

Trouble did not thank me for saving one of her nine lives or any of her kittens' lives. She spat at me and began to herd her family away.

The men, even Sven, were glad to see the cats.

I took the burlap sack back to the cat drum. Trouble didn't think much of me right now, but I knew how much she liked the burlap bag.

I found her standing at the drum entrance, as if she were waiting for the sack before beginning housekeeping again.

I got on my hands and knees to spread it, when something caught my eye at the far end of the drum—a package wrapped in canvas. Maybe it contained some leftover food I had brought on board, and I could give it to the cats.

Then I remembered—it was the rhubarb jam I had carried from the Faeroes.

I tore off the wrappings. The jar was unbroken. I raced to the cabin with it. The men were drinking cold coffee and eating a skimpy breakfast of flatbread. I set the jam on the table as if I were offering a pot of gold.

"RHUBARB JAM!" Thompsen shouted, wide-eyed.

"Where did it come from?" the skipper asked.

"From the Faeroes," I said. "I intended to eat all of it myself on the way to England."

Ruud reached for a spoonful. "A day for small miracles— a strange bird comes calling—cats come to life—and now rhubarb jam appears."

"There are no *small* miracles," Kristiansen said, piling his flatbread high with the red gold sweet.

"True," Sven said. He raised his coffee cup to me. "I am alive. It all adds up to one *big* miracle. *TUSEN TAKK*." A thousand thanks—from Sven to me. A miracle!

16

SEAMAN LUNDE

The rhubarb jam was the last good food we ate.

I helped Olaf salvage the remaining supplies. "The bread is moldy," he said. "Cut off the green."

Once this would have turned my stomach. Now I tried not to waste a crumb.

There were still a few potatoes—small, wrinkled culls.

"Mind you peel carefully, so as not to waste any," Olaf cautioned.

I had a better idea. "We can cook them with the skins on."

When we found a few pounds of dried peas in the bottom of the locker, we cheered as if we'd discovered a box of jewels, even though we had no salt meat to cook with them.

"How many more days?" Olaf asked me.

I kept track now on a calendar I had made. I pulled the

cardboard out of my pants pocket. "According to the captain, ten more days and we should smell land."

Olaf let out a whistle. "We will all be skeletons by the time we reach North America."

"We're getting to the end of the coffee," I said. One of my jobs was to grind the coffee beans.

Olaf sighed. "The men will miss coffee even more than potatoes. We will ration it—coffee for breakfast and for men going on watch."

I began marking each passing day with an X on my calendar. By the time I got to "seven days from land," we were out of everything but fish cakes and flatbread.

That evening, at supper, Sven and Thompsen argued about the oil.

"It will not last long enough," Sven predicted.

"It will hold out—just barely—if we are correct in our calculations," Thompsen said.

Someone suggested a game of cards, and I went up to the wheelhouse. Kristiansen was helmsman. He was the least experienced of the crew, and secretly I believed I could handle the *Bergholm* better than he. But I was just a boy and not given a chance.

The sea was fairly calm. The sun was a red gold half circle on the horizon. Something caught my eye to starboard—a persisting glitter in the sea.

I pointed it out to Kristiansen.

He shrugged. "Just the sun reflecting on the water."

I got the binoculars and looked at it. Was it a reflection? Did I imagine that the thing took on shape—roundish with pole-like arms?

I handed the binoculars to Kristiansen and took the wheel while he scanned the sea.

"A mirage," he said, taking over again.

"There is something out there," I insisted, taking another look through the glasses.

Kristiansen grinned. "Maybe it's Sven's sea serpent."

"Let's tell the captain," I said.

"You tell him. I don't see it. You do."

I wanted to. Still, more than anything, I hated laughter from the crew.

Then I remembered what the doctor had said: "When you think you see the unusual in the usual, then you must make a decision. It is real, or just a mirage?"

I went down to the cabin.

The captain was busy over some figures. I hated to butt in. I stood next to him, shuffling from one foot to the other.

He glanced up. "Well, speak up," he said.

"Sir, sir, I think there is something unusual to starboard," I said.

He was on his feet.

So were the cardplayers. Nothing unusual had happened in days.

I was right behind the captain going into the wheelhouse. "Where?" he asked, taking up the binoculars.

I pointed, but now I was unsure. The sun was lower now. I could not see the object without the glasses.

The captain looked for some minutes. I thought he must be annoyed with me. Instead, he ordered Kristiansen to change course.

As we approached the object, I saw that it was just an old piece of metal. I was sorry I had told the captain about it; so I was amazed when he gave the order to stop alongside the mangled contraption.

"It looks like it's from a downed plane," he said.

The skipper agreed. "It looks like a gasoline tank. See the aluminum fixtures on the outside."

"Some poor pilot is at the bottom of the sea," Thompsen said.

"We'll take it on board," the captain said.

After it was hoisted to the deck, Sven eyed the huge mass gloomily. "What good is it?"

The captain had a satisfied look on his face. "I'll tell you what it's good for. Now we've got something to barter with when we reach land. You men gave me what money you had to help pay for the oil we needed. This will make up for it. We've got several kilos of copper here."

He started to walk away. Then be bellowed, "Well done, Lunde."

Who was he talking to?

My name was Lunde, but only members of the crew were called by their last names. He turned and looked straight at me. "Well done," he said again.

I suddenly felt six feet tall! A broad-shouldered, first-class Norwegian seaman.

17

COLUMBUS AGAIN

The first sea gull came on the sixteenth day.

I had just begun to dish up a poor breakfast of fish cakes and water when Olaf stuck his head in the cabin door. "Columbus is back," he shouted.

The men pushed from the table and bounded to the deck. I raced after them.

There, on top of the mast, looking exactly like our old friend Columbus, a sea gull stood on one leg.

Shouts went up from the crew.

"Shades of Noah's Ark," Kristiansen said.

"Canada ahoy!" Ruud yelled from the steering house.

The commotion brought a prediction from the captain. "We're no more than five days from land," he announced.

That evening, after supper, he was pelted with questions.

"Where in Canada will we land?"

"Will the people speak English or French?"

"Will they welcome us?"

The captain spread out the atlas map. With his thumbnail he creased a line along the southern edge of Newfoundland. "We will land somewhere along the coast of Nova Scotia. Where, exactly, depends on our oil."

As usual, Sven groaned at the mention of oil.

The captain pinpointed a dot on the map. "Here is Cape Race, on the tip of Newfoundland. Unless my calculations are off, we should see the Cape Race light sometime during the night five days from now. There must be no delay in spotting it. Because of our oil situation, we cannot afford an error."

His head came up sharply and his cool gaze sought me out. "Lunde," he said.

"Yes, sir," I said, straightening my shoulders.

"Lunde, you have keen young eyes and good judgment. I want you on deck that night."

I was too stunned to even nod.

From that moment on, I thought of practically nothing but the Cape Race light.

I forgot about the gnawing hunger and the thirst I felt most of the time. I was a man and could bear such trifles as the rest of the crew did. I was the one entrusted to find the Cape Race light.

How would I know it?

I worried.

The next day the captain called me up to the steering house. "I'll tell you all I know about the Cape Race light," he said. "It's a flashing white light, and its range is nineteen

— 78 —

nautical miles. That means you can see it at sea level at that distance.''

Nineteen miles. I tried to remember how far that was on land. I knew that a nautical mile was just a fraction longer than a land mile. How could I identify a light nineteen miles away?

"The important thing to remember," the captain went on, "is that the light has a two-second flash every 7.5 seconds. Do you know now how to count seconds?"

I nodded.

"There is a horn on Cape Race. It sounds every thirty seconds in low velocity. You might not hear it, however."

After that I practiced counting seconds. The skipper had lost his watch during the storm. The doctor's had been damaged. The captain's could no longer be relied upon. My count would be critical.

Each day I marked our progress on my calendar:

THREE more days . . . nine sea gulls today
TWO . . . . Sven says oil very low.
ONE . . . . My eyes play tricks.
                       I imagine I see houses,
                       people, animals.
TONIGHT IS THE NIGHT!

I worried all day.

What if fog hides the light?

What if I miss it? I remembered a story I read long ago about a disaster where a ship went on the rocks because the lookout had mistaken a lamp in a cottage for the lighthouse light.

It was the longest day.

Night finally came.

The skipper's face, as he guided the *Bergholm,* was barely visible in the faint light of the steering house.

The sky was packed with stars—every one of them seemed to blink.

Once I shouted, "I see it!"

"Just a falling star," the skipper said. "You'll see the loom of the light before you see the actual light."

I made myself turn away from the stars, and I went on deck and stood at the rail.

I felt something rub against my leg. Trouble. In the dark, her eyes shone like twin blinking lights. Everything blinked, even Trouble.

And then I saw a strange glow. Was it the loom the skipper had told me about? Like a moonrise on the horizon.

I waited for the light.

My skin crawled with nervousness, and my fingers, grasping the rail, were clammy with sweat.

Then I saw the tiny point of light. It flashed like a diamond and then was gone.

Had I seen a star?

There it was again.

Gone!

If it's the Cape Race light, it will have a two-second white flash every 7.5 seconds of darkness, I reminded myself.

I must count.

FLASH—one, two.

Dark.

FLASH—one, two.

Count the darkness: DARK—one, two, three, four, five, six, seven plus seconds. FLASH—one, two seconds.

Again I counted.

This was it!

"CAPE RACE," I shouted up to the skipper.

"CAPE RACE," I yelled as I ran through the cabin door.

The captain hurried to the wheelhouse to take the watch.

The men rolled out of their bunks.

We stood on deck, astounded that we had indeed succeeded in crossing the Atlantic. The captain's calculations had been on target.

I did not want to go inside to sleep. I rolled up in a blanket on deck.

I felt good about myself for having identified the light.

As I closed my eyes, I could smell trees—balsam and spruce—although we were miles from land. I heard a low moaning sound. It had to be the horn on Cape Race.

The *Bergholm* had made it.

18

IN THE JUG

When I awakened, we were coasting along a rocky shore thick with evergreens that came right down to the water's edge. Crew members stood in knots, pointing, talking excitedly. How could I have slept through any of it?

"Where are we?" I asked, coming up to the doctor and Kristiansen.

"Nova Scotia," the doctor said.

Kristiansen, dressed in knickers and a bright sweater for the occasion, gestured toward the shore. "This is the forest primeval. The murmuring pines and the hemlocks . . ." he said.

The doctor smiled. "We're off *Ar*cadia, not *A*cadia."

"I know," Kristiansen said. "But it reminds me of Longfellow's sad poem."

The men were in a jovial mood.

Ruud whistled. "Land—mud—how great it is."

Thompsen threw his cap into the air. "Solid ground—I'm going to kiss it."

We were in the Bay of Fundy, the doctor told me. "We'll be docking soon in Yarmouth. See, we're coming into it now."

I looked out over green lands, fat sheep grazing, bright farmhouses.

I couldn't get enough of looking.

We dropped anchor in the harbor.

Immediately a motorboat, with two uniformed men on board, was alongside.

Everything happened fast after that.

The uniformed men vaulted onto the *Bergholm*.

Something was wrong.

The conversation between the men and the captain and skipper did not appear to be friendly.

The skipper strode over to us. "The Yarmouth police are taking us into custody."

Sven groaned. "That means the jug."

And so we found ourselves, on this first day in the land we had struggled so to reach, in a small room, wondering what would happen next.

I didn't have my land legs yet. The room seemed to move up and down, the same as the *Bergholm* had.

"It's demeaning," the captain spluttered.

"Outrageous," Ruud shouted.

"Understandable," the doctor said calmly. "Canada is at war, and we are an unidentified boat."

"You will be turned over to the Royal Navy for questioning," the police told us.

And so we were. One at a time.

When it was my turn, I was so scared I would say the wrong thing that my voice quaked when I told how I had stowed away on the *Bergholm* because I wanted to reach my family in England.

It took three days before we were cleared by the Norwegian government in London.

The officer who gave us the good news was friendly. "Why don't you strapping young men join the Canadian Navy?" he asked.

Our captain was brisk. "We will have a meeting to decide what to do."

The meeting was held back on the *Bergholm*. "We've been invited to stay in Canada if we wish," the captain explained. "There are war jobs to be had. You can join the Canadian Navy. Every man makes his own decision. But after our reception here, I'm not for Canada."

The doctor interrupted. "Canada is at war. A strange boat would have been treated the same at home in Norway."

Stoneface didn't mellow. "I have made my decision," he said. "I am taking the *Bergholm* to New York City."

"NEW YORK!" the skipper shouted, jumping to his feet.

"We have no oil," Sven said.

The captain grinned. "I have bartered the gasoline tank we salvaged for oil and provisions."

Now everyone talked at once.

The captain held up his hand. "There is a Norwegian Consulate in New York City. Some of you will probably want to get back as close to Norway as possible. I have heard there are Norwegian freighters in New York harbor carrying supplies to England. There is a chance they can use qualified seamen. Each man decides for himself, but the *Bergholm* goes to New York. Who wants to go with her?"

To a man, the choice was New York.

Excitement was in the air as the crew made ready to sail. Only Sven was grumpy. "The New York police will question us, as the police did here. We'll be in the jug again."

"The United States is not at war," the doctor reminded him.

The joy of the crew at the prospect of going to New York City was not contagious insofar as I was concerned. I felt all hollow inside, as if I were losing everything. The men would find jobs, go their separate ways, but what about me? What would happen to me?

"Hey!" Ruud shouted. "What's the first thing you're going to do in New York?"

"Get a bath," Kristiansen answered. "How about you?"

"Me?" Ruud said. "I've been wondering what American girls are like."

"Not many blondes," the skipper said.

"The Ziegfeld Follies for me," Olaf said. "Hey, supper's about ready. No fish cakes tonight."

The talk about New York continued over the meal. "I know what I'm going to eat in New York," Sven said. "A hamburger and a Coca-Cola. That's what Americans eat. I read that somewhere."

The skipper turned to the doctor. "How about you? What's New York got for you?"

The doctor's eyes lighted up. "The Great White Way. I want to walk all the way from The Battery to Times Square." He looked up at me as I poured tea into mugs. "Jon, how about taking that walk with me?"

"I guess so," I said.

I went out on deck as soon as I could. I wanted to bawl. I did not want to leave the *Bergholm*. It was home. The crew was my family. They were all I could count on. I couldn't go back to Norway. I didn't know if my parents were alive in England, and I had no way of reaching there. I was afraid of the United States. I was lonelier than ever.

And yet, it was my mother's country. My father had spent two years in America, had met my mother out West somewhere. They were married and he had brought her to Norway.

My Norwegian grandmother was afraid they would leave Norway one day and go back. So whenever "the States" were mentioned, she would tell me about the bad things there—gangsters, policemen wearing two guns, the depression.

"What's a depression?" I once asked her.

"Men out of work. They sell apples on street corners to get money for food."

Once she took me to a Wild West moving picture. "See what goes on in America?" she said.

The United States was surely a place to be wary of. I borrowed the doctor's atlas and turned to the map of the United States. It was so big it spread over two pages.

"It's three thousand miles from the Atlantic Ocean to the Pacific Ocean," I announced to the crew, who were in the midst of a card game. "Its population is 131,669,275."

"Unbelievable," Ruud exclaimed. "In all Norway there are only three million souls."

The United States was indeed a monster wearing a ten-gallon hat and with two guns slung about its waist.

19

THE MODERN
LEIF ERICSSONS

I was not prepared for what I felt when I first glimpsed the Statue of Liberty.

I had stayed up all the warm summer night, waiting to see the lights of New York City.

We arrived in early morning. There, directly in front of the *Bergholm* stood the big, strong lady. She seemed to welcome me personally.

The *Bergholm* was flying the Norwegian flag. I felt a great pride in her as she *chug-chug*ed her way through the busy harbor.

A U.S. Coast Guard vessel came alongside and signaled us to follow.

Had Sven been right? Were we going to be put in custody again?

The Coast Guard officers were smiling, waving. One of them clasped his hands together and shook them over his head.

A tugboat blew its siren at us.

"Strange," the skipper said. "We are not in their way."

The Coast Guard led us to what was called "the 27th Street Pier." Alongside stood a big factorylike building. BETHLEHEM STEEL was painted on its side. My mother had taught me English, and so now I could read the signs all around us.

A man with a camera sprang at us as soon as we docked.

"Who are you?" the doctor asked.

"A reporter from the *Sun*. Been waiting half the night to scoop your story."

"How do you know about us?" the doctor asked.

"From the radio," he said.

The Coast Guard officers came on board. They shook hands with us. "We've been looking for you," they said.

"How did you know?" the doctor asked.

"The Canadian Navy alerted us."

More newspapermen came.

We did not know what to make of all this.

A man strolled alongside the *Bergholm* and shouted, "I hear you came all the way from Norway. Is that so?"

"We crossed the ocean," I shouted back.

"In that boat? All the way from the war zone?"

"It's a great boat," I said.

More people came.

Soon there was a crowd.

The captain, who had gone to the Norwegian Consulate, came back waving a newspaper. We crowded around to look.

There, right on the front page, was our story. The headline read:

MODERN LEIF ERICSSONS TO ARRIVE

The story told how we had escaped from the war zone and crossed the ocean in three weeks. It told of the hurricane, sixteen-foot waves, the iceberg, our lack of food and water. It made us look like heroes. The crew had a hearty laugh about that.

In the afternoon, another newspaper headlined the story. There were pictures of the "sturdy Vikings who had crossed the Atlantic without nautical charts, and with only a school atlas to guide them."

One of the newspapers even printed a picture of Trouble and the kittens.

Men, women, and children came to see the *Bergholm*. First a trickle. Then a crowd. On the second day, thousands came.

They came with fruit.

With vegetables.

With meats.

With candy. Salt-water taffy was the best of all, I thought.

Members of the Norwegian-American Society came—from Manhattan, Brooklyn, Jersey. "You must have dinner with us," they urged. They brought herring—goat cheese— *lefse*—"to make you feel at home."

Our decks overflowed with oranges, bananas, soft drinks.

"Beer in *cans*," Sven marveled. "Who ever heard of beer in cans?"

"This is America," Ruud said. "Everything happens here."

A group of musicians played Norwegian folk songs.

Six children came with food for the cats. They had collected money in their neighborhood to buy it.

The Norwegian Consulate introduced us to U.S. money. I learned that a "buffalo" was a nickel. "Two bits" meant a quarter, and a "cartwheel" was a silver dollar. I also learned to say *Okay!*

SO THIS WAS THE UNITED STATES.

I felt like crying and laughing at the same time.

A Norwegian freighter captain came to the *Bergholm*. He shook hands all around. "My ship is bound for England soon. I can use good Norwegian seamen."

I sat, scared, as some of the crew signed up—Thompsen, Ruud, Kristiansen, Sven.

Not Olaf. He had telephoned a cousin in the state of Minnesota. He was going out there.

"This is a big country. It will take three days by train to reach Minnesota. Where will you get that much money?" Sven asked.

Olaf's face split in a grin. "They have already wired it to me. This is a land of miracles."

It was not a land of miracles for me. I knew the Norwegian Consulate had tried to locate any relatives of my mother living in this country, but with my meager information about them, they had not been successful. They had sent a cable to England to try to find my parents, but they had little hope of an early reply.

The captain did not sign up to go back on the freighter. "I must stay with the *Bergholm* until it is decided what to do with her," he said.

The skipper was the last one to sign on the freighter.

Now there was only the doctor left.

"How about you?" the skipper asked.

The doctor pulled an envelope from his jacket. "I am mailing this today—an application to serve in 'Little Norway' in Toronto. I heard about it when I was in England. Young Norwegians are being trained there for the Norwegian Air Force. I understand they can use doctors."

Everyone's life was decided. All but mine.

I knew the men talked about my problem when I was not around. I knew it worried them. But I had brought it all on myself. What could I do about it?

The freighter captain was a big hulk of a man—almost seven feet tall, with a windburned, craggy face and the biggest hands I'd ever seen. I was a little afraid of him; but the next time he came on board, I tackled him.

"How about giving me a job on your freighter?"

"A boy!" he exploded. "How can I take a boy on my ship?"

Ruud spoke up. "He is my son. He must go where I go."

This time it didn't work as it had with the submarine commander. The freighter captain dismissed Ruud's comment with a wave of his hand. "Your papers state you are twenty-seven. Were you then a boy father?"

The crew had a good laugh at that.

"Jon is an experienced cabin boy," the doctor said. "He can cook, clean up, and even lend a hand at the helm. Surely you need someone like him on your ship."

The captain shook his head. "What was such a young boy doing on your voyage?"

"He thought we were going to England," the doctor explained. "He hoped to find his family. He was separated from them because of the war. He stowed away on the *Bergholm.*"

"Stowed, you say?" The captain looked at me with an appraising Norwegian eye. "So you had the nerve to stow away on board this fishing smack? That would not be possible on my ship. Not possible."

I felt a lump in my throat.

"Unless," the captain said, one eyebrow cocked, "unless it were tried in the early morning, let's say one or two o'clock, when there's only one man on guard, a sleepy one at that."

I couldn't believe what I had heard.

The crew did. They gave a lusty Norwegian *"HURRA!"*

The lump in my throat got bigger. I was going to blubber right in front of the men. I dashed for the deck. I stopped short. Trouble sat in my path, eyeing me accusingly. I had forgotten about her and the kittens. What would happen to them?

The kittens were cute, already weaned, and many a visitor to the *Bergholm* had begged to have one of the kittens born on the smack. The kittens would be no problem.

But no one had asked for Trouble.

I carried her into the cabin and stood in front of the freighter captain. I didn't even have to tell him what was on my mind.

He shook his head. "No cats."

"How can I leave her?" I asked.

The captain's face closed up.

I bit my lip.

Then I glanced at the crew—the ones who were going on the freighter—Sven and Ruud, Thompsen and Kristiansen. I detected a look of conspiracy in their eyes. Four would-be smugglers.

Maybe it was not fair to the captain, but Trouble would earn her keep. Freighters had rats, I'd heard.

20

FROM THE BATTERY
TO TIMES SQUARE

It was our last day on the *Bergholm*.
She was polished and painted. The brass was shined.
The crew had packed their belongings.
Good-byes were being said.
I felt sad.
"Jon," the doctor called to me. "We've one more thing to do."
"What's that?"
"Our walk up Broadway. Let's go."
I was eager.
As we walked along, I listened to the blend of voices—French—Italian—Polish—Irish.
We stopped to buy hot dogs from a pushcart. "Be sure to see the World's Fair," the vendor urged as he stuffed buns

with sausages and slathered them with sauerkraut. "I'll tell you just how to get there. You see that bus . . . ?"

We wondered how he knew, with all the milling people about, that we were strangers.

We ate, gawking up at buildings so tall they scraped the sky like mountains.

We looked in the windows of a store called Macy's and one called Gimbels, and we marveled at the displays of toys, food, and clothing.

I saw a watch on the sidewalk and picked it up. "Look what I've found," I said to the doctor. "All it needs is a new crystal."

A passerby smiled and stopped a moment. "It's worth only a dollar. Throw it away. Buy a new one."

What a country.

We bought buttered popcorn and threw some to the pigeons in Times Square. I remembered Sven scolding me when I threw fish cakes to the gulls. Here there were no shortages. There was a wonderful feeling of plenty.

At the end of the workday, we found ourselves in a crunch of people streaming out of offices and stores, rushing toward taxis, double-deck buses, subways.

We ate supper at an automat. Was there anything one could not get? All one had to do was put a coin in a slot and out would come a sandwich, a hot dinner, or apple pie.

Marvels! Marvels!

The Great White Way dazzled us. One electric sign after another:

ZIEGFELD FOLLIES — QUAKER OATS — IVORY SOAP — COCA-COLA — Some signs winked and blinked and magically turned into pictures before our eyes.

We stood in the middle of the sidewalk and looked and looked, and were jostled on all sides.

I felt so alive, so buoyant my feet didn't touch the sidewalk.

Tonight, Trouble and I would stow away on board the Norwegian freighter. But one day, after I'd found my parents, I would come back. I would see my mother's country from one end to the other.

One day when the war was over.

ONE DAY!

Kanske?

No *maybe* about it.

For SURE.